RACCOON RAMPAGE

RACCOON RAMPAGE

ANDREW COPE

Illustrated by Nadia Shireen

BARRON'S

First edition for the United States published
in 2013 by Barron's Educational Series, Inc.

Text © Andrew Cope 2012
Illustrations © Nadia Shireen 2012

First published in 2012 by
HarperCollins Children's Books
77-85 Fulham Palace Road
Hammersmith, London W6 8JB

All inquiries should be addressed to:
Barron's Educational Series, Inc.
250 Wireless Boulevard
Hauppauge, New York 11788
www.barronseduc.com

ISBN: 978-1-4380-0302-3

Library of Congress Catalog No.: 2012955323

Date of Manufacture: February 2013
Manufactured by: B12V12G, Berryville, VA

Printed in the United States of America
9 8 7 6 5 4 3 2 1

For Sophie and Ollie.

And, no, before you ask,
you can't have a pet raccoon!

Chapter 1

The Raid

The moon was bright and everything in the forest was still. All the action was at Max's place. Rocky couldn't help but worry. "It's b-b-breaking and entering," he stuttered, pointing at the broken window. "What if the old man hears us?"

Quickpaw's head poked out from a litter of cookie wrappers and he wiped crumbs from his whiskers. He stood up, dusted himself off, and burped. "We'll clean up before we leave," he said. "Max won't know anything about our little raid." He moved along the shelf and examined a tin. His reading wasn't the best, but he could recognize a picture of a salmon when he saw one. "Gotcha!" he squealed. "Guys, a tin of our favorite fish!"

Sunshine looked up from his meal, cat food smeared around his mouth. "Cool! Nice find, boss," he chomped.

Dempsey had scarfed down so many apples that his tummy was hurting. He was prowling the top shelf in search of something that always made him feel better—muffins.

"B-But what about Max?" hissed Rocky. "We shouldn't be here, sneaking around his shop in the dead of night. He'll get upset, you know."

"Stop fretting," scoffed Dempsey from up above. "Max is snoring. And he'll never hear us, so long as we're quie—" The small raccoon brushed against a bottle. It wobbled. Dempsey gulped. He was very high up. *Not good!* He reached to steady the bottle and made things worse. His paws went to his eyes as the bottle fell, smashing on to the concrete floor. All four members of the Hole-in-the-Tree gang froze. Dempsey peeped out from behind his claws. "Sorry!" he whimpered. "Maybe Max is a heavy sleeper?"

Light flooded from the crack under the door. All eyes went to Quickpaw. "What do we do, boss?" squeaked Rocky. "I told you we'd be in trouble."

"Hide!" instructed Quickpaw, leading by example and diving into a sack of oatmeal. Instinctively, the three other raccoons found hiding places. Dempsey

 squeezed behind a jar of pickles on the top shelf; Sunshine wiped the cat food from his mouth and leaped into a boot; Rocky

looked around frantically. All the hiding places were taken! Max's footsteps were coming down the stairs. The old man was grumbling. "Either robbers or raccoons," Rocky heard him mutter. "Either way, they'll be in trouble." Rocky's panic nearly boiled over as he heard the storekeeper walking down the hallway.

Rocky remembered casing the joint. There was something that Max called a "cash register." He remembered Max pressing a button and a little drawer shooting open. *Just enough room for a raccoon,* he hoped.

Max's hand was on the door handle as Rocky pressed the button. The cash register opened and he dived in. The drawer closed and the room fell silent.

Max barged through the door, flicking the light switch as he entered. It was three o'clock in the morning and his eyes were as wild as his hair. His brain began putting the clues together. *Broken window. Glass on the floor.* His old-fashioned general store was very cluttered and he figured there were a lot of places for a robber to hide.

"Come out, come out, wherever you are!" wheezed the storekeeper. "Anyone burgling Max's store is going to get what they deserve." The old man shuffled his slippered feet to the end of the aisle, crunching on the broken glass as he walked. He jumped around the corner, ready to catch an intruder. Quickpaw sank deeper into the oats; Sunshine scrunched himself into the foot of the boot and held his breath as the man stalked by; Dempsey dared to peer down from the top shelf. Max was wearing blue-and-white-striped pajamas and a very angry face.

The raccoons heard a distant voice. "Anyone there?" shouted Max's wife from the safety of the bedroom.

"We'll see soon," muttered the store-keeper to himself. The old man hauled open the door of his storage room and peered inside. He pulled the cord and the storage room light came on. Dempsey gasped from behind the pickle jar. *Boxes and boxes of food. A whole treasure trove that we've never discovered! Next time*, he promised himself. *If there is a next time!*

Max seemed calmer. The old man assured himself that whoever had tried to rob his store had disappeared into the night. And, from what he could gather, nothing seemed to be missing. He was pleased that he'd scared them away. "Better check the register," he croaked. Dempsey's eyes widened as the old man approached Rocky's hiding place; Quickpaw's eyes and nose poked out of the sack; Sunshine's black-and-white face twitched out of the top of the boot.

Max shuffled behind the counter. His bony finger pressed the cash-register button and the drawer sprang open. Max was used to the satisfying ker-ching noise.

But his eyes widened in horror as a screaming black-and-white animal hurled itself at him. Man and beast yelled. Max staggered around the room as he tried to yank the furry intruder from his face. Rocky clung on. Their

scuffle sent them flying into a shelf, knocking over and shattering the jar next to Dempsey, splattering pickles against the wall. *Yikes!*

Dempsey was first out of the door. Quickpaw made for the window, cutting himself as he fled. Rocky was peeled from the man's face and thrown to the floor. The raccoon was winded. He looked at the shocked man while he got his breath back. *It's now or never!* Rocky got away, and scooted toward the door. The terrified raccoon then darted through the legs of Max's equally terrified wife.

"Burglars?" wailed the lady.

"Worse," growled her husband. "Thieving raccoons. And if there're any left in here, I'll find them!" he said.

Sunshine was out of the boot. He was flat against it, weighing the odds of making it to the window. He eased one foot from behind the boot and heard Max exclaim, "There's one!"

He heard the old man's slippers shuffling toward him and he eased around the other side of the boot. "Come out, you varmint," coaxed the storekeeper.

Sunshine tried to think clearly. He picked up a tin of salmon and hurled it across the room. Max twirled and looked in the direction of the noise, hoping to catch his intruders. Sunshine sniffed the air. He could smell a chance to escape. He knew he didn't have much time. Max was distracted, so this was his moment. The raccoon's sharp eyes fixed on a barrel near the door. He wasn't sure what "live bait" meant, but he liked the look of the picture. *Wiggly worms!* The raccoon crept across the floor. He dodged the wooden splinters and sprinted for all he was worth. Max was close, but he made it to the barrel, chest heaving. With a mighty shove he managed to push the barrel over. It hit the hard floor and the lid fell off, wriggling worms oozing into the room. The lady screamed and fainted. The floor was alive and the old man slipped. His slippers came off and his toes squelched. He tried to get to his feet, but slipped again, onto his hands and knees in a sea of worms.

Sunshine played it cool. The raccoon smoothed his whiskers and straightened his hat. He loved his trusty cowboy hat. He took a plastic bag and filled it with apples before sidestepping the worms and making his way out into the night.

He stood at the door and saluted the old man. *Respect Max*, he thought. *You* came close. But I think we can chalk this one up as another victory for the Hole-in-the-Tree gang.

CHAPTER 2

Daydream Believer

His friends were waiting for him as Sunshine scampered up the redwood tree and hauled himself into the hole. He pulled the bag in and apples spewed out onto the floor. He high-fived Quickpaw, then Dempsey and Rocky. "Borrowed these off Max on the way out," he said, crunching into a juicy apple.

"I thought you were a g-goner," stammered Rocky.

"He was no problem," exaggerated Sunshine. "Remember, this raccoon can break into and out of anything," he said, cracking his tiny knuckles. "You've heard of a cat burglar? Well, guys, meet the world's best raccoon burglar!" he bragged, bowing to his friends. "Oh, and young Rocky-me-boy, I thought your hiding place was excellent, by the way."

Rocky smiled with pride. "I collected these," he said, holding out some gold and silver coins. "They were in the drawer. They sure are pretty. Humans use them to swap for stuff. So maybe next time we can swap instead of steal?"

Quickpaw Cassidy was the brains behind the operation. He knew Max was on to them. In fact, the whole village was on to them! He looked around their den. It was carpeted, courtesy of bathmats from Maggie's Gift Mart. There were four small cushions to sleep on. Quickpaw smiled as he remembered this particular raid. *Off the sofa at number twenty-three. We had a nice drink of lemonade too. And some candles from there.* Then there were the toothbrushes from the mini-market.

Mmm, being chased from there by a man with a golf club was a bit hairy! And the mirror, he thought, his chest swelling with pride.

Our biggest and best job to date. He glanced at his reflection, his shiny black eyes smiling. *That took all four of us, working as a team. We risked seven years of bad luck getting it down from that first-floor window!*

The law of the forest meant that no animal could survive on its own. The Hole-in-the-Tree gang worked well as a unit. They were still very young raccoons, but they were learning fast. Quickpaw was full of daring ideas and he knew the others looked to him for direction. And, as the biggest, he was always expected to be at the front if there was trouble. He'd recently stood up to Calamity Colin, the roughest, toughest, and meanest raccoon in the forest. Luckily for Quickpaw Cassidy, he could count on his friend The Sunshine Cub and together they'd fought off "The Calamity." *A shame about Sunshine's tail, though*, thought Quickpaw. *Still, half a tail is better than none!*

His tail aside, Sunshine was the coolest raccoon in the forest. He even used the fight with The Calamity to his advantage, exaggerating to make it sound like he'd fought off a pack of wild dogs. When everyone else went into panic mode, the gang could count on Sunshine to stay calm. And added to that, Sunshine could break into anything. He'd even broken into the police station and stolen a walkie-talkie that sat proudly next to the mirror. Sunshine liked the mirror, never missing an opportunity to spruce up his whiskers and straighten his cowboy hat. Sometimes he'd press the walkie-talkie button and jabber away in Raccoon to the police. From the tone of their reply, he knew it annoyed them. But it was great fun!

Rocky was the worrier, always predicting bad weather, predators, and famine. He was skinny and nervous and would flinch at the slightest noise, but was good to have in the gang because he nagged the others until things got done. It was Rocky who'd insisted they build their den high enough to avoid bears. It was Rocky who insisted on a small stash of food "for a rainy day," and it was Rocky who'd made sure they didn't steal honey from the killer bees.

In fact, Rocky was the perfect antidote to Dempsey, who saw the bright side of everything and the good in everyone. Dempsey was also a bit of a dreamer. He loved to sit and watch Max's TV through the window and he dreamed of a new life in the city. His stash of *City Life* magazines was stacked neatly in one corner of the den and he'd plastered the walls with pictures of skyscrapers. So when Dempsey said they should move to the city and get an apartment with a TV and Xbox, it was important to have Rocky around. He was the sensible one. "We're raccoons," he would say. "We live in the forest. In trees! It's what raccoons have always done and what they always will do! And we should be cautious."

Like all good leaders, Quickpaw was a good listener. *Maybe Rocky had a point?* Quickpaw knew there was a fine line between being cautious and being daring. He also knew there was a fine line between being well-fed and starving. While their tummies were full, courtesy of Max's General Store, he knew that winter was coming and they needed to put on weight before food became scarce.

Quickpaw Cassidy cut through the excited chatter. "We need to do one more big job," he said to his gang. "Something that will get us enough food to see us through the winter."

"B-B-But—" began Rocky.

"No buts," snapped Quickpaw, waving his paws for calm. "You see this," he said, jabbing at his tummy. "It's not fat enough to keep me going in the winter. Have you guys felt the temperature change? Snow's coming."

"Which means frozen ground," agreed Sunshine. "No grubs or fruit."

"And the lake will be iced over," continued Quickpaw. "So no fish."

"No fish!" Rocky whimpered. "Disaster. I love fish."

"Then listen carefully," said Quickpaw, "because I have a cunning plan."

CHAPTER 3

Something Fishy

"We've got until the sun reaches its highest point. That's when the van arrives. Is everyone clear on the plan?"

"No *problemo*," purred Sunshine. "I steal the keys. Easy for a raccoon with such nimble fingers as these," he said, waving his paws. "And I open the back doors."

"And me and Quickpaw collect as many fish as we can," piped up Dempsey. "Then away into the forest with enough supplies for the entire winter season. It's genius!"

"More like dangerous," began Rocky. "Max is sure to be on the lookout for us," he shivered. "And it's not fair to Max, is it? I mean, it's stealing."

"Max'll hardly notice if a few fish go missing," sighed Quickpaw. "Humans have plenty of food. And look at what they're doing to the forest. Remember our last tree house?"

Rocky gulped, recalling the horror when their tree house was destroyed to make way for some apartments.

"We lost everything. Plus, humans are always fishing on our lake. That's stealing too. They'll be emptying it if we're not too careful."

"It's not empty," argued Rocky.

"Not yet," agreed Sunshine. "Think of this job as our last one of the season. We nab a few fish from the back of the van before Max gets them into his freezer. The old boy will never notice. He'll be happy that his freezer is full. And we'll be happy that our winter stores are full."

"And our tummies," beamed Dempsey, rubbing his furry belly.

"Plus," chipped in Quickpaw, "we can leave old Maxy-boy alone. He can have winter in peace, without us starving raccoons breaking and entering."

Rocky still didn't look sure, but Quickpaw knew there wasn't time to stand around persuading him. Yes, it was a risk. And yes, they had to be extra careful. And yes, it was their biggest heist ever. But as leader, he had responsibilities to the gang. And his chief responsibility was to keep them alive through the barren winter season. "All back here for midday sun," he barked.

"And guys," he sniffed, "be careful out there."

Quickpaw and Dempsey worked as a pair. They'd already stolen Max's clothesline, a long string of freshly washed shirts, socks, and pants trailing in the dust. They'd identified their next target, the hammock on Mr. McCluskey's porch. "It's good and sturdy," suggested Dempsey, "plus he's only four doors from Max's so there won't be far to travel." They approached the cabin, sniffing cautiously. Dempsey stood on his hind legs to get a better view of the hammock. They knew McCluskey had a dog and Quickpaw was keen to keep his bushy tail intact. Rocky was positioned high, clinging to the top branch of an oak. Quickpaw's words were ringing in his head—*Being on lookout is a very responsible position. Lives depend on it.* It was no wonder his tiny raccoon teeth were chattering.

Rocky looked to his right and saw Quickpaw and Dempsey approaching the cabin. All seemed clear. He looked left and watched the fish van winding its way slowly along the road. "Right on cue," he muttered. "Let the action begin."

Quickpaw went first, darting across the no-man's-land of McCluskey's garden and under the wooden veranda. He beckoned to Dempsey. *So far, so good,* sighed Rocky from above. *Now get that hammock.* He shouldn't have worried. Quickpaw had already made a start, gnawing at the rope that was holding the hammock up. Dempsey started at

the opposite end,

holding the

rope in

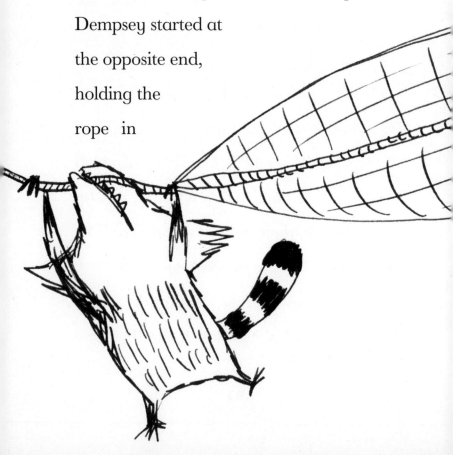

his tiny
hands, his
razor-sharp teeth
chewing frantically. The
raccoons were halfway through the
ropes when the door creaked open and
McCluskey appeared, a soda can in his
hand. The raccoons scuttled out of the way

while the rather large man stretched and sipped the rest of his soda. He crumpled his empty can and threw it into the yard. Rocky heard the massive belch from his treetop-lookout position. *Yuck!*

Quickpaw peered up at the man. No way, he thought, as McCluskey moved toward the hammock. *You can't lie there. We need it for our project!*

McCluskey stood and scratched a while, contemplating how he would attack the hammock. Getting in was always a bit tricky. He decided that one big lunge would do it. Rocky gulped as he watched the man leap into his hammock. The half-chewed ropes snapped and McCluskey fell to the floor with a thump. "What the—" he began, climbing to his feet and examining the ropes. "Someone's sabotaged my hammock!" Suspecting a practical joke by his son, Mr. McCluskey stormed inside. Dempsey and Quickpaw heard furious yelling as they leaped onto the porch and clutched the hammock in their tiny paws.

Perfect, thought Rocky. He glanced left and saw the fish van pulling up at Max's store. The driver was getting out and going to see Max. To his right, there were two raccoons sprinting for their lives, a hammock trailing behind, and a clothesline trailing even further.

The Sunshine Cub had waited patiently. He'd burrowed underneath Max's store and his beady eyes shone with excitement. *The keys*, he sniffed. *My mission is to get those keys.* So, as the driver temporarily left his van, Sunshine went straight in. He dived through the open window and stared at the buttons and levers. *Wow!* he thought. *Gadgets! This is so cool.* He sniffed the fishy smell coming from the back of the van and it brought him to his senses. His little raccoon fingers clasped the key. He twisted it. *Nothing. It's stuck.* He could hear shouting from the McCluskeys' house. He could see Max and the van driver chatting in the store. Sunshine twisted again, pulling at the same time, and the keys came away in his paw. The light-fingered raccoon crept out of the driver's window, leaped onto the windshield, and up onto the top of the van. He waved to Rocky in the lookout tree, the keys glinting in the sun. *Now for the tricky part.* Sunshine shimmied down the opposite side of the van and clung onto the back door. His other hand fumbled for the key and tried to fit it into the lock.

Rocky had seen enough. It wasn't looking good. McCluskey and his son had spotted the missing hammock and were coming after the raccoons. From what he could see, McCluskey was waving a baseball bat and shouting angrily. Even worse, Max and the van driver had finished chatting and were making their way toward the van! *I'd better go and help*, he thought, his panic turning a downward climb into a fall.

Quickpaw and Dempsey knew they didn't have much time. They arrived at the van just as Sunshine had unlocked the back door and swung it open. "Ta-da," he bragged, revealing more fish than the team had ever imagined. The hammock was laid flat and Quickpaw and Dempsey got to work. Quickpaw was inside the van, tossing fish out; Dempsey was catching them and laying them on the hammock. "Quickly, quickly," shouted Rocky, panting after his run. "They're coming! Too late," he squealed as Max looked up and saw the team at work.

"No way!" shouted the storekeeper. "Pesky varmints stole my money and now they're thieving my fish!"

"And my new hammock!" yelled McCluskey, breaking into a trot.

Rocky's panic had gone into overdrive. He leaped up and down, his screeching loud enough to be heard by the whole town. The hammock was only half full, but they could wait no longer. Dempsey and Quickpaw tugged with their claws and started to drag it into the forest. A whole winter's supply is heavy!

While the world whirred crazily around him, Sunshine did what he did best—he stayed calm. McCluskey was coming at his friends with a baseball bat. *Not good.* And Max was striding toward the fish van in angry mode. *Also pretty dire. I need a distraction,* he thought. The quick-thinking raccoon slipped back into the van and pushed a few buttons. The horn blared and windshield wipers swished at full force. The van driver looked horrified as he spotted a raccoon in the cab. Sunshine pressed a few more buttons, nearly deafening himself as music blasted from the speakers. *What does this one do?* The windows whirred down. Then back up. *Nice!* He opened the glove compartment and found some mints. *Mmm, yummy,* he thought, popping one into his mouth. *But hot!* he discovered, wafting his paw at his mouth.

Sunshine's beady eyes fell on a lever with a red button. *Wonder what this one does?* He pressed the button and the handbrake was released. The van started to roll backward, slowly at first, but gradually accelerating. Sunshine had done his job. He looked out of the window. The crowd was now chasing the van instead of the raccoons. He leaped from the door and

scampered into the tree line. He watched
his gang tugging the hammock of fish
one way, while the small crowd chased
the van the other way. His paws went to
his face as the van toppled over the bank
and splashed into the lake. There was

a hissing and fizzing as it filled with water, followed by a *glug-glug* as it disappeared. *At least the fish have been returned to their rightful resting place,* he thought, before turning and chasing after his friends.

CHAPTER 4

No Surrender

It wasn't hard to follow the fishy trail. By the time Sunshine got back to the redwood tree, Quickpaw had set up a pulley system. The clothesline was dangling from the tree house. One of Max's favorite shirts was tied to the bottom and

Rocky was loading fish
inside. Quickpaw and
Dempsey were pulling
the fish upward, emptying
the shirt, and sending it down
for a refill. Most ingenious,
thought Sunshine, full of
admiration.

Then his senses prickled;
he stood on his hind
legs and listened.
The ground
was vibrat-
ing. He
concentrated
hard.

Barking. And footsteps. "Quick, team," he warned, "all raccoons back to base immediately!" There was a scratching as Sunshine and Rocky shimmied up the trunk and into the hole. Dempsey was hauling the clothesline up as the posse arrived at the base of the tree. Max yelled something, presumably about seeing his shirt and pants disappear into a hole in the redwood. Dogs were barking. The raccoons fell silent, their chests heaving after scampering up the tree.

"What shall we do?" asked Rocky, his face twitching nervously. "Should we give ourselves up? And maybe return the fish?"

Dempsey chuckled. He looked at the fish piled up in the corner of their den and licked his lips. "Keep quiet," he said, "and everything will be alrigh—"

The gang's eyes filled with horror. It took Max two pulls of the cord before the chainsaw roared into life. He revved it, like a giant bumblebee.

Rocky gulped. "I remember that sound," he said. "This isn't good at all."

The peace of the forest was being destroyed by exhaust fumes and noise. Rocky hung his head out of the hole. The den was halfway up the tree, a nice big hollow with a large branch to step out onto. There was a group of humans at the base of the tree, and two dogs were straining at their leashes, yapping furiously. All faces were looking upward. Fingers pointed at Rocky. "There's one!" yelled a voice. "I can see his thievin' raccoon face. And where there's one, there'll be more. Let's do it."

The chainsaw whined as its teeth cut into the bark. Rocky gulped as bright, creamy yellow sawdust began to spew out. "The men are chopping our tree down!" he babbled. "Our home. Our lives. It's all over."

"Grab what you can," ordered Sunshine, snatching one of Max's woolly hats from the clothesline. Quickpaw went for a fish; Dempsey grabbed a copy of his favorite magazine, *City Life*; Rocky stepped into a pair of Max's underpants and tied them in a knot so they fit snugly around his waist. He tucked some silver coins inside for good measure.

"Quickpaw, any ideas?"

The raccoons looked on hopefully as their leader calmly took a deep breath.

"Two options," he said matter-of-factly. "Step out onto the branch, paws in the air, and surrender. We then go down the tree and they'll set the dogs on us."

Rocky squealed with terror. "One hundred percent dead!" He wafted his face with his paw in an attempt to cool down. "Not the dogs," he said. "Please, please, there has to be a Plan B."

"Or," said Quickpaw, "we take our chances and escape." He popped his head out to remind himself of the distance between their tree and the next. "Too far to jump right now," he said, "but if we climb higher and time things right, we can jump as the tree is falling. Claws out, guys. This is going to be risky!"

Four sets of sharp claws were extended and the raccoons bundled out of their den and scaled the tree as high as they could go.

They looked down at the humans. Yellow sawdust was still pouring from the tree as the chainsaw chomped its way through two hundred years of growth. The forest canopy spread out below them almost as far as a raccoon eye could see. A river snaked into the distance.

Then, just for a moment, all went quiet. The silence was followed by a creak, then a groan, as the giant tree began to sway. Rocky's teeth were chattering. He pulled a few coins from his pants and threw them away. No point in having unnecessary weight while I attempt the jump of my life, he thought.

"Timmmbeeerrrr!" yelled Max's voice from below as the fall started to gather pace. There was another painful groan as the giant redwood twisted and fell. The Hole-in-the-Tree gang clung tightly to each other, the world around them tilting. "Not until I say!" yelled Quickpaw above the rush of leaves. "Hold your nerve." The oldest and tallest redwood smashed against the branches of other trees as it toppled. "NOW!" yelled Quickpaw Cassidy, and the Hole-in-the-Tree gang leaped for their lives.

Chapter 5

The Leap of Faith

Rocky's pants saved him. The others found him dangling from a branch. He'd taken a whack in the face and was unconscious, but they unhooked him from the branch and gently lowered him to the forest floor. The gang could hear men shouting and dogs yapping. Quickpaw was the strongest. He passed the fish to Sunshine and loaded the lifeless Rocky on to his back. The gang set off into the forest. It was slow going and the dogs were getting closer. "And," panted Sunshine, "hungry."

Eventually Quickpaw's knees buckled and he collapsed to the ground, exhausted. A brown dog bounded through the undergrowth, its teeth snapping in anticipation of a raccoon lunch. The quick-thinking Sunshine hurled his fish toward the dog and it stopped to munch the easy meal. By the time the dog had finished, the raccoons were gone. Sunshine and Dempsey hauled Rocky to a nearby tree and hung his body over a low-hanging branch. The other raccoons sat in the leaves, their chests heaving, but their breathing silent. They watched as the dog sniffed the forest floor before it bounded onward toward the river.

"Phew, close one," whispered Sunshine as another dog scampered past, nose to the ground. Dempsey climbed the tree to assess the situation and gather his thoughts. They were in serious trouble. He could see at least a dozen men combing the area. *Plus dogs*, he thought. *It's only going to be a matter of time before we're discovered.*

The river is within striking distance, though. Maybe we can get across to the other side.

Dempsey returned to his friends and told them it was best to carry on. The raccoons took turns carrying Rocky as far as the edge of the cliff. The forest stretched out behind them and the river flowed below. They'd reached the end of the chase. They laid the still-motionless Rocky out on the floor and slapped his face. Nothing! "Is he, you know..." said Dempsey.

"Of course he's not 'you know,'" said Sunshine. He pulled at the elastic of Rocky's pants and stretched it as far as it'd go. Then he let go and the *snap* roused the

67

groggy raccoon. "Ouch!" he said opening his eyes. "Have I died?"

"Not yet," hissed Sunshine. "But by the sound of those hounds, you soon will. We all will!" He leaned over the cliff and took in the scene. Way below was the white water of the icy river cutting its way through the valley. He walked along a fallen tree to take a closer look; there was a sheer drop below. "It's like a diving board, guys," he said. "But it sure is a *loooong* way down!"

"Well, there's absolutely no way…" began Rocky as the dogs arrived at the cliff. There were three of them, brown-and-black canines of pure muscle and aggression. Slobber hung from their mouths as if they hadn't eaten for a week. "...that I'm going to be eaten by a dog!" He ventured farther out along the fallen tree, followed by Sunshine and Quickpaw. The four raccoons edged their way forward, walking the plank. The river raged below. "We die if we stay—and we die if we jump!" whimpered Rocky.

Quickpaw considered the options. He'd never dived into a river before, but he'd seen humans do it. He peered over the edge of the fallen tree and looked at the swirling rapids below.

The dogs stalked closer, their saliva running ever more freely. *Fresh raccoon*

for supper! A man came out of the trees. He was wearing a checked shirt and jeans, and on his head was a raccoon-skin hat. Quickpaw Cassidy stared at the headgear. He immediately recognized the tail that hung down from the hat. "Calamity Colin! He's wearing The Calamity!"

That was it as far as Quickpaw was concerned. He always considered that the best leaders weren't big on words, but on actions. He put his paws above his head like he'd seen humans do and fell head first toward the river. The others watched in awe as there was a small splash below.

Dempsey just held his nose and jumped. "A leap of faith! Wheeeeeeeeee!" One of the dogs ventured onto the fallen tree. Sunshine pulled his cowboy hat down over his eyes and dived for his life, his legs flailing and a terrified yowl piercing the air. Rocky hated water. He backed up as far as he could go. The dogs were wary, choosing their footsteps carefully.

Rocky looked down at the torrent below. *Humans wear trunks a bit like mine,* he thought, pulling his pants up and giving himself a wedgie. The sight of the gushing river made his tummy churn. *It's now or never,* he decided. *The Hole-in-the-Tree gang must stick together through thick and thin.* He wasn't sure if this moment was thick or thin, but either way he attempted a dive, wailing pitifully as he toppled toward the rapids.

Chapter 6

Four Minus One

Rocky's pants filled with water and dragged him under. He kicked as hard as he could, spluttering to the surface. He caught hold of a log and his claws sank in. Dempsey was behind him, bobbing up and down like a cork.

Sunshine and Quickpaw were nowhere to be seen.

As Rocky's legs pumped, his energy reserves were emptying. There was a terrific noise up ahead and the raccoon cub strained his neck above the water. *Rapids—and then a waterfall!* He kicked harder, but it made no difference, the river was too wild. Rocky was helplessly twisting and turning as the white water tossed him around. There were jagged rocks everywhere and the tiny raccoon kicked his hardest, sucking in lungfuls of air whenever he got the chance.

Just as Rocky thought he was done for, a paw swooped down and caught him by the pants. Quickpaw hauled his half-drowned friend into the safety of an overhanging tree. Dempsey was next, hauled by his fur, spluttering and coughing up water. The exhausted raccoons lay on the branch of a tree. The river raged below, water thundering over the falls. "At least we're alive," panted Quickpaw.

"Has anyone seen The Sunshine Cub?" The raccoons raised their weary

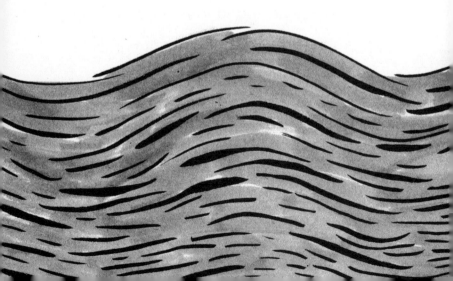

bodies and Rocky scrambled higher up the tree for a better view. Dempsey and Quickpaw heard a squeal and they followed Rocky's paw. His bony finger pointed to Sunshine's cowboy hat cascading over the waterfall.

Sunshine woke. It was getting dark and he was very cold. He could hear the river

roaring by and his keen raccoon senses soon kicked in. He spat out a mouthful of gravel and sat up, his eyesight gradually adjusting from double to single vision, but he could still hear water in his head. He sniffed... *Barbecue? Fish?*

Sunshine hauled himself to his weary feet and shook, water spraying everywhere. He limped to the water's edge and dipped his paws in the icy river to wash his face. His hat was sailing by so he braved the water once more, wading in and grabbing it before retreating to the safety of the shore. Sunshine cocked his head to the side and shook. *Ahhh, that's better*, he thought, as a warm trickle of water flowed out of his ear. He punched his hat back into shape and placed it on his head. He straightened his whiskers and spiked his fur. *Feeling like a super-cool raccoon again!* He was shivering. *Must get some food*, he decided. *And quick!*

Sunshine limped into the woods, following the smell of barbecuing fish. Something glinted in the moonlight and he bent over to inspect it. He picked up a stick and prodded the jagged metal teeth.

The animal trap snapped shut and the raccoon jumped backward in alarm. His stick was eaten up, trapped in the jaws. *Nasty. A raccoon could get hurt in one of those!* Sunshine limped on, being extra careful, his nose leading him toward the possibility of food. Before long, he stumbled upon a clearing lit by the orange glow of a camp fire. Four men were huddled around it, one strumming a guitar, the other two yowling along. Sunshine's eyes were drawn to a large fish, skewered on a stick, cooking over the embers. He scanned the scene and put his calm thinking skills into action. The men were staring at the fire, the radiance lighting their orange faces. Smoke and sparks rose into the twinkling night sky. In the semi-darkness behind them was a tent and a four-by-four Jeep. Sunshine resisted the urge to go for the fish. *Too obvious.* Instead, he circled the camp and snuck into the tent. He sniffed their sleeping bags, nearly fainting as his super-sensitive nose came across some sweaty socks. He backed out of the tent and leaped into the open Jeep. *That's more like it!* he thought, as he munched on sandwiches and chocolate bars. His tummy full, Sunshine curled up in a spare sleeping bag and settled down for the night. Tomorrow he would find his friends.

CHAPTER 7

A Shot in the Dark

Quickpaw led the remainder of his gang down the tree. Rocky spent a few minutes scraping sand out of his pants, but elected to keep them on. "Sunshine liked my pants," squeaked Rocky. "He told me they made my tail look bushy."

He wiggled his backside and turned to glance at his black-and-white tail that stuck proudly out of a hole in the back of his pants. "And besides, it's the best place to keep my coins," he smiled, shaking his hips harder so his pals could hear the clinking.

The three raccoons sat silently on the riverbank and watched water cascading over the falls. "Maybe he survived," suggested Dempsey. "He could be down there catching fish and having a great time."

Rocky looked away from the force of the water and sobbed. He knew that no creature could survive that fall.

"Whatever happened to our friend, you can be sure he was cool and calm, right to the bitter end," said Quickpaw. "And he'd have wanted us to be cool and calm too. We need a plan, guys. And quick."

Dempsey jumped up and ran to the riverbank. "My *City Life* magazine!" he yelled, holding it up for the others to see. The soggy magazine was open at a picture of a penthouse apartment in New York City. "That's where we should go," exclaimed Dempsey, jabbing a paw at the page. "Sunshine would have said 'Go for it!' There's nothing left of our house and let's face it, if we ever return home,

Max and his posse will have us strung up. I bet there are 'Wanted' posters out for us. We're fugitives."

"Outlaws!" smiled Quickpaw, liking the idea. "Taking from the rich and giving to the poor."

"Er, I don't think that's quite what we do," commented Rocky. "We take from Max and the villagers to feed our faces and furnish our den."

"Exactly," said Quickpaw. "They're the rich and we're the poor. Poor little starving critters."

Dempsey flicked the page. The raccoons gasped. "Look at that kitchen…and those recipes."

"And a hot tub!" grinned Quickpaw, rubbing his tiny hands together. "Like our lake, but piping hot. Imagine? Sunshine used to say that the streets of the city are paved with food. Everything a raccoon could want. Hot dogs, doughnuts, burgers, spaghetti..."

Rocky was slobbering. His tummy made funny squeaking noises. "OK, guys," he snapped. "I'm running on empty. We're fugitives. We're 'wanted' raccoons so we can't go home. The question is, how do we get to the city?"

"People," suggested Quickpaw. "Find people and they will have transportation."

"And food," reminded Dempsey. "And maybe when we get to the city we can open a hotel for raccoons called 'The Sunshine Hotel' so our pal is never forgotten."

It was dusk. The raccoons felt energized as they scampered through the night. Sunshine may be gone, but his memory was well and truly alive. Eventually they came across an orange glow in the forest. "Fire and warmth," observed Rocky.

"And food," drooled Dempsey, stepping forward. "Let's go and help ourselves to that yummy fish."

"Not so fast, buddy," warned Quickpaw, sizing up the scene. Four men were sitting around a crackling camp fire. One was strumming a guitar while the others sang along, country and western wailing into the night sky. Sizzling on a spit was their prize—a large fish.

Quickpaw's mind whirred. He indicated toward a trap. "Careful gang," he warned, pointing to the metal jaws, "there may be a few of these scattered around. Let's see if I can catch these humans at their own game. I'll distract them. You guys go for the fish."

"Is that it?" said Rocky. "It doesn't sound very…you know…*clever.*"

"It'll be clever enough when your belly's full of smoked salmon," barked Quickpaw. He waved his paw as a signal to his friends to keep out of sight. Then, in his capacity as boss of the Hole-in-the-Tree gang, he circled the men, waiting for the right moment. He leaped out of the shadows and stood on his hind legs. "Cooeee, guys," he barked. "Over here. It's me." He slapped his thigh. "Anyone for a tasty raccoon steak?" The men looked up, pointed at the raccoon, shared a joke, and carried on singing. One of the men turned the fish to cook on the other side, the smell wafting through the clearing.

Quickpaw began to do jumping jacks. "*Hellloooo!*" he barked. "Stop pointing. Start chasing?"

The men looked again, a little startled to see a raccoon doing something they'd only ever seen on exercise DVDs. One of the men got up and walked to the Jeep. He rummaged in the back and came out with a net. "Let's get ourselves some raccoon meat to go with the fish," he grinned to his companions.

Quickpaw was very familiar with nets. The men were now standing and the mood had gotten serious. "We ain't caught nothin' all day," said the man with the net. "We even had to buy the fish from Max's. And all of a sudden supper turns up, doin' aerobics!"

"Guess it's our lucky day," said his friend, pulling his pants up over his large belly.

Quickpaw retreated a little, tempting the men away from their camp fire. They followed, hypnotized by the prospect of an easy catch. Quickpaw Cassidy gulped. The man came closer with the net. The raccoon sank into the shadows and a powerful flashlight picked him out. Another gulp. *Not good.* His plan was starting to not seem so clever. There was a loud *snap* as he stepped backward onto a twig. The man charged toward him, swinging the net and catching it on a low tree branch. "Did we get him?" yelled one of the hunters.

Not quite, thought Quickpaw, sprinting into the darkness. His heart was thumping as he heard the man free his net and continue to chase him. Quickpaw wished Sunshine was around. This was time for a cool head. The metal jaws of the trap were glinting in the moonlight. *A few more steps*, thought Quickpaw. And *wham!* The raccoon winced as the trap snapped around someone's foot. There was a yell. Quickpaw heard men scuffling in the undergrowth as they tried to pry their friend's foot from the trap.

Dempsey heard the yelling and came out of the shadows, sniffing furiously. *Barbecued fish, but no people.* He tiptoed toward the barbecue, Rocky close behind. Dempsey grabbed the kettle and hauled it to the fire. "Help me," he barked. Together the raccoons tipped the kettle, water pouring onto the hissing flames until eventually the orange had been replaced by smoky blackness and gray ash. Rocky was reaching for the fish when they heard a voice from behind.

"OK, varmints," warned the voice. "Turn around with your paws up."

The man's eyes were wide with surprise. It wasn't every day that his camp was

raided by a racoon wearing pants. Rocky's

beady eyes were also as wide as they'd

ever been, but with fear. He dropped

the fish and turned to face the mouth of the net. As his life flashed before him, something else flashed down from the tree. Something attached itself to the man's chest. Something black and white. Rocky noticed it had half a tail—"Sunshine!" he yelped. The man screamed. The hunter howled in pain as he fell over a rock, startled by Sunshine. Dempsey and Rocky made their escape. Sunshine let go of the man and followed his friends into the forest.

The raccoons had enjoyed the fish, but now they needed transportation. They had circled the camp several times, assessing the situation. There was a lot of hobbling. One man had a trap attached to his foot. Another was heavily bandaged from his fall. The injured men were loaded into the back seat of the Jeep. The driver and his friend hauled themselves in and set off for the hospital.

The Hole-in-the-Tree-gang sat in the back of the vehicle, snuggled in a sleeping bag. Sunshine grinned to his friends. "The gang is reunited," he beamed, "and we're getting a free lift to the big city, where there's going to be a raccoon *rampage!*"

CHAPTER 8

City Life

The raccoons woke as the Jeep stopped. Quickpaw was the first to peep out from the sleeping bag. "Wowza," he reported back. "It's just like the picture!"

The wounded men were helped from the vehicle and wheelchaired toward the

Accident and Emergency entrance. The huge hospital towered above them, higher than the tallest tree in the forest. It was the early hours of the morning and the city was awash with twinkling lights. "More than the stars at night," gasped Quickpaw. "It's so beautiful."

On the other side of the road were houses, and beyond them, skyscrapers. "Hardly any trees," noticed Rocky. "But loads of tall mountains of light!"

"And loads to eat," sniffed Dempsey, taking in the smells of nearby fast-food joints. "The city is going to be great!" There was no time to leap out. The driver pulled away from the curb and four sets of raccoon eyes peered at the night sights as they ventured deeper into the big, bad city.

Eventually, the Jeep stopped and the man climbed out. His camping trip hadn't quite gone as planned and he was weary after a night with no sleep. The raccoons watched him go through the door of a house. A light came on and then, after a minute or two, off it went again as the man slumped into his bed. "The sun's coming up," smiled Dempsey. "Let's explore!" The Hole-in-the-Tree gang hopped down from the back of the Jeep and crept into the man's yard. The first rays of sun were peeping over the horizon and the city was quiet. "He's got a tree!" shrieked Rocky with glee, running to the man's small apple tree and hugging it tight. "I love trees!"

Dempsey was already sitting on the swing, rocking himself back and forth. "Check this out," he said. "A fair ride for raccoons."

"And there's another ride over here!" shouted Sunshine, leaping onto the trampoline. "Wheeeee!" he yelled, springing as high as he could. "I'm nearly as high as the apple tree!" Dempsey joined him and they jumped together for a few minutes, thinking the city sure is a fine place for raccoons to be. Dempsey

got carried away and nearly bounced off the trampoline. His claws came out to steady himself and there was a huge ripping sound. Both racoons fell through the black material, landing in a laughing heap on the grass. "Cool game," chuckled Sunshine. "Let's see what else the city's got."

By the time Rocky, Dempsey, and Sunshine got to the back of the yard, Quickpaw was already in the hot tub. He'd found a button that made it bubble. "Like relaxing in the lake," he said, as his gang jumped into the warm water.

"But much warmer than the lake," noted Dempsey, settling his body into the bubbling water. His eyes closed and he sighed with pleasure. "I think we might have found raccoon paradise after all!"

"We need to eat," decided Quickpaw after a while. "Maybe there's some fish in that big pond over there." The sun was now shining, and the swimming pool glistened invitingly. Quickpaw got out of the hot tub and shook himself before wandering over to the pool. He dipped his paw in and scooped up some water to drink. "Yuck!" he said, spitting it out. "Tastes horrible. The humans must have done something to the water to deter raccoons from drinking it."

What's this? he wondered, approaching a soccer ball, sniffing and touching it cautiously. The ball rolled forward. "Nice one." Quickpaw ran up and kicked the soccer ball as hard as he could. It sailed through the air and there was a tinkling of glass from next door.

The raccoons stiffened as a black-and-white animal walked along the garden wall. They had never seen a cat. She looked at the raccoons and walked on, like cats do. She had the same markings as the raccoon cubs, even down to the white whiskers. They watched in open-mouthed amazement as the cat disappeared through a hole in the door.

"What was that?" asked Rocky nervously. "Did you see that funny raccoon creature vanish into that wooden thing, like magic? What if it's a special raccoon with superhero powers?"

"You're the superhero, buddy," noted Quickpaw. "Superheroes always wear their pants on the outside. Come on, let's check it out. Maybe that weird-looking raccoon knows where there's food!"

The soggy raccoons scampered to where the cat had disappeared. A small door was cut into the larger door. "How very amazing," remarked Sunshine, marveling at the idea. He pushed at the cat-flap and it squeaked back and forth.

His head peered through. He sniffed. His black nose turned to his friends, a smile on his raccoon lips. "Coast's clear…and I smell breakfast!"

Sunshine hopped through the cat-flap, onto the luxurious carpet. He dug his claws in. *Oooh, what a lovely feeling,* he thought. *I'm going to like living here.*

Dempsey squeezed through next, followed by Quickpaw. Rocky's nose peered through. "Guys," he hissed. "Not sure we should—what if there's danger?" It was too late. Quickpaw grabbed Rocky's ears and yanked him through the cat-flap. "Much more danger out there," he explained. "We're a gang; we stick together."

The house was quiet, except for Rocky's chattering teeth. The strange raccoon was curled up on the sofa. She eyed the intruders, but couldn't be bothered to move. The gang tiptoed toward where the strongest smells were coming from. "Woohoo! A kitchen," squealed Dempsey, leaping at the fridge door and attaching himself to the handle. The door swung open and he was inside. "Butter. Yogurt," he said, dipping a paw into a carton. "And pickles! My fave." He tossed an egg to Quickpaw, who caught it expertly. He sheared off the top of the egg with his razor-sharp claws and downed it in one gulp. Dempsey was enjoying himself in the fridge. He chucked an egg at Rocky, who was so nervous that he missed it, and it splattered on the floor. *Oops!*

"*Cheeeese,*" squealed Dempsey, throwing a huge lump of cheddar to the gang. "And cake..."

Sunshine was sitting on the chair, eyeing the cat. "You're a funny-looking raccoon," he said. "Are you a city version?"

Raccoons and cats are distantly related somewhere in the evolutionary chain, but their languages are entirely different. The cat meowed back and Sunshine looked shocked. "You sure have a bad throat, sister," he remarked. He turned his attention to the TV remote. Sunshine couldn't resist gadgets. Ever since he'd stolen the walkie-talkie from the police station he'd loved buttons. *And check this one out,* he purred to himself, examining the remote. *Red, blue, green, yellow. And I wonder what this big one does?* Sunshine jabbed a paw at the button. For a moment, nothing happened. Then all of a sudden, the huge screen on the wall started talking. *Yikes, what's that? Too much noise,* he panicked. He jabbed at a few more buttons, accidentally turning the volume higher. The TV switched between morning news and cartoons, then settled on a music channel.

The noise was deafening to the raccoons' sensitive ears. Dempsey peered

out from the fridge. "What's going on?"
he yelled. "I can't hear myself think,
never mind eat!" Dempsey's foot caught
a milk bottle and it toppled from the
fridge. Two gallons of white stuff flooded

FRIDGE-O

the kitchen floor. "That was a massive smash—sorry!" apologized Dempsey. Cornflakes fell from the cabinet where Quickpaw was nosing around. Rocky sniffed the combination. "These crispy things work well with milk," he said, lapping at the floor.

Meanwhile, the man hadn't slept all night. And now, just as he'd got into bed, his kids were up early and bashing about downstairs. "Will you keep it down!" he yelled. "I do not want music on full blast at six a.m.!" His head went under his pillow, but the bottle smashing on the floor was the final straw. He fell out of bed and reached for his robe.

The raccoons' ears pricked up and they exchanged glances. *Humans!*

The man's daughter had beaten him to it. A straggle-haired little girl wandered down the stairs, rubbing sleep from her eyes. She was wearing pink princess pajamas and was dragging a teddy bear by its leg. She saw the raccoons and brightened up. "Cuties," she said, starting to skip downstairs a bit faster. "New pets! And one of you little critters has got pants on. He's my favoritest!"

By the time her dad had found his slippers, the raccoons had made an exit, hiding in the dirty laundry basket in the basement. The little girl was sitting at the breakfast table, drawing pictures. Milk, cornflakes, and eggs littered the floor and music was blasting from the TV. Her father was angry, but softened when he saw his little girl kicking her legs and singing to herself. "What are you drawing, honey?" he asked, looking over her shoulder. "Looks like a raccoon," he smiled, inspecting the picture more closely. His face creased into a frown. "But with pants on?"

CHAPTER 9

A Pizza the Action

The basement was warm enough, but the raccoons soon got bored of hiding. As Quickpaw reminded them, "We've got a whole city to explore!" Sunshine tried the door handle. He rattled it as hard as he could. He twisted and turned it, but had to admit defeat. "No good, guys," he admitted, "someone's locked us in." Eight raccoon eyes scoured the room for an emergency exit. The basement had no windows and it was full of clutter. A washing machine stood idle and a faucet dripped into a sink. Quickpaw Cassidy scraped at the drain where the washing machine was attached. He beckoned to Sunshine. "A job for you," he grinned. Sunshine found a spoon and scraped away at the drain. The gang stood back and watched as he used the spoon to open the iron grid— then a black hole opened up in the floor. It reminded him of something he'd seen on Max's TV. "In case of emergencies," he said, "all raccoons should follow me through the nearest exit." He disappeared into the tunnel, the gang in hot pursuit.

It seemed forever before they stopped. The raccoons had scooted through the city's underground drain network, turning left and right so many times that they were truly lost. They got used to the darkness, but not the smell. One tunnel had been full of rats, so they'd turned back. "Rats are evil creatures," reminded Quickpaw. "Never, ever trust a rat!"

The gang halted under a shaft of light. Shadows passed overhead and it was noisy up there. "But at least there's daylight," suggested Dempsey sparkily. "Let's go upstairs and see the city from ground level." Sunshine stood on Quickpaw's shoulders and removed the grid. He hauled himself out and then helped his friends, pulling them up from the drain. Cars and buses whizzed by as the four small raccoons backed up against the curb. They'd emerged from the storm drain at the side of a main road. "It's a bit hectic," observed Rocky as a bus sped by, sending a massive splash of water their way. "But look over there," said Quickpaw. "I don't know what that writing says, but I'm loving the picture!" A huge pizza lit up above Mario's Bistro, stringy cheese oozing from a cutaway slice. "Anchovies, pepperoni, salami...anyone for extra tuna?"

"But the traffic," warned Rocky. "We'll get squished," he said, pointing to a frog imprinted in the asphalt.

"Our friend didn't pay attention," suggested Quickpaw. "Have you noticed? When that light turns red, all the traffic stops. That gives us tons of time to cross to pizza heaven."

Right on cue, the light went red and Quickpaw stepped into the road. He scampered halfway before the traffic erupted again. He waited patiently for the cars and trucks to stop before he made it across to the other sidewalk. Quickpaw stood on the opposite side of the road and waved. Then he jabbed a paw to the pizza parlor. "See you in there, guys," he mouthed. "Extra tunaaaa…!" he yelled, his voice trailing away behind a truck.

Sunshine was next, timing his run to near perfection.

Dempsey wasn't sure Rocky would dare make the trip on his own, so they teamed up. While Sunshine's calm brain enabled him to think things through, Rocky's panicky approach made things much more haphazard. The traffic stopped, but he wanted to be absolutely sure there was no more before he stepped off the curb. He looked right…then left… then right and left again…then down at the squashed frog. Dempsey was across the first lane. He looked back and Rocky was doing one final check. *Left. And right. Seems clear. One last check…*"Come on, slowpoke!" urged Dempsey, but it was too late. Rocky had decided the coast was clear at almost exactly the same time that the lights turned back to green. Engines revved and the line of traffic raced forward. Rocky was in the first lane. He looked up and saw cars bearing down on him. Dempsey sprinted back and grabbed Rocky by the paw. He held his other paw up, sure that it would halt the traffic. There was a blare of horns and screeching tires as cars swerved to avoid them. "Stop!" screeched Dempsey, standing tall, "Raccoons crossing!" Rocky wasn't looking. He made himself as small as he could, his arms wrapped around his black-and-white head and his tail curled under him. A car narrowly missed the raccoons, its tires roaring by, inches from them. Dempsey dragged his friend to the left to avoid a bicyclist. He heard the ringing of a bell and the bicyclist fell. Then, more horns blared and the

raccoons heard the crunching of metal as cars collided.

Then, all of a sudden, the traffic seemed to stop. *Right over us! What a coincidence!* thought Dempsey. Rocky's face came out from behind his paws and he saw he was safely under a bus. He saw feet appearing everywhere as drivers jumped out of their cars. He heard arguing, each driver blaming the other. The bicyclist kicked a man who'd knocked her off her bike. "Road hog!" the raccoons heard her yell.

With pandemonium above, Dempsey was able to lead his friend through the tangle of vehicles. *This is easy peasy*, he thought as he caught up with Sunshine and they skipped across the rest of the highway to grab a share of the pizza action. *These humans don't seem too bad after all. It was really nice of the traffic to stop for us just like that.*

Luigi was in his kitchen. It was a busy lunchtime and the pizza ovens were going full throttle. Waiters and waitresses buzzed in and out of the kitchen, giving and collecting their orders. Quickpaw Cassidy and The Sunshine Cub peered in through the kitchen window, marveling at the inside. "Humans just seem to eat and eat," noted Quickpaw. "It's no wonder there are so many big ones!"

Rocky and Dempsey joined them at the window. They soon worked out the logic of the kitchen. A small man was busy chopping; another was swirling dough in his hands, turning it into large circular shapes; someone else was smearing the round things in red stuff and laying out ingredients. At the end of the production line was a large oven.

All eyes went to Sunshine. "Looks yummy," said Dempsey. "What's the plan?"

Sunshine scratched his ear, deep in thought. "I suggest we avoid the oven at all costs," he said. "That table looks best," he declared, pointing his paw at the chopping board where small piles of onions, ham, and pepperoni were arranged. Tubs of tuna and pineapple sat there, tantalizing the hungry raccoons. "And mushrooms," said Dempsey, his eyes going gaga.

Sunshine lowered the window and beckoned Rocky through. "You're the smallest and skinniest," he said. "So you've got the best chance of going unnoticed. This, young Rocky Raccoon, is your moment!"

Rocky was shaking so much that the loose change in his pants was clinking. "But..." he began, "what if—"

"What if nothing," snapped Sunshine. "We're here to support you. Jump onto the table, grab whatever you can, and you'll get away before they've even noticed."

He gave his terrified friend a little push of encouragement and Rocky fell off the windowsill onto the chopping board. The chef was busy looking at his order, so didn't notice a raccoon stuffing salami and pineapple into its pants. He raised his knife, its metal glinting in the sunshine, and was about to bring it down when he saw the raccoon. "*Mamma mia!*" yelled the man, "ther's a rat in di kitching," he said, his accent making the words sound strange to the raccoons. He couldn't stop the momentum of the blade and it slammed down next to Rocky.

The raccoon didn't feel anything, but instinctively knew that something was wrong. He leaped for the window, scrambling to escape, but his balance was wrong. A woman was screaming and lots of men were shouting some very fast words. Outside, the gang felt helpless as Rocky tapped frantically at the glass, his paws struggling to hold on. They watched as he lost his balance and fell backward, back into the kitchen. A man smashed a saucepan down, narrowly missing Rocky's head. A rolling pin came next, smashing a plate to smithereens. Then a lady appeared, brandishing a broom. Rocky was on the countertop and she swiped at him. He jumped and the broom smashed into Luigi's face. The gang watched in horror as their furry friend dashed through a few legs before disappearing into the restaurant itself. The troop moved to the next window to watch the action unfold. Rocky was leaping from table to table. It was like a silent movie, the customers' terrified faces telling the story of Rocky's raccoon rampage.

Quickpaw winced as a chair smashed down near Rocky. Luigi had joined the action, slapping a rolling pin menacingly in his hand. Rocky disappeared under a tablecloth, customers squealing as a raccoon ghost trailed across the floor. Then the ghost hit a wall and stopped dead. *Ooomph!* Luigi was there in an instant, smashing his rolling pin down onto the tablecloth. Luckily, he missed the lump and Rocky was away once more, a black-and-white blur sprinting from under the cloth. As customers streamed out of the front door, Rocky saw his chance. *Upward!* He bounded onto a chair and then a table. The next jump was the biggest. He made it, swinging from the lampshade. There were more screams as the raccoon swung, Tarzan-like, scooping a slice of Hawaiian pizza on the way past. He sat on the window ledge and surveyed the scene. Luigi was shaking his fist and the man with the chopping board was holding up something that looked like a black-and-white feather duster. Rocky's face fell as he glanced behind at where his bushy tail should have been. The loose change clinked in his pants, but there was no tail. He sobbed. Then, as the waitress was apologizing to the few remaining

customers, he realized that Luigi was coming at him again. *This is no time to feel sorry for yourself,* thought Rocky. He stuffed the pizza into his pants and disappeared out of the window.

By the time the gang reached the storefront, Rocky had retreated across the road and they just saw his white pants disappearing back down into the storm drain.

Sunshine looked at Quickpaw's stripy tail; he'd always been jealous of its fullness. His own half-tail had always eaten away at his pride. But as he saw Rocky's bare bottom disappear down the drain, he realized that having half a tail was better than none at all!

CHAPTER 10

Raccoon-napped

"**Y**ou did it, Rocky!" congratulated Sunshine. His friend sat shivering in the darkness, whimpering about his lost tail. "Never mind about the chopping-board incident. You filled your pants with food and that's mission accomplished! We get to eat because of your bravery."

The gang chomped happily, all except Rocky. "My beautiful tail," he wept. "I really don't like the city at all. We're not the Hole-in-the-Tree gang anymore, we're the Lost-in-the-Poo-Pipes-Underneath-a-Concrete-Jungle gang. Tail-less, hopeless, and pointless," he sniffled.

With supper finished, the raccoons ambled their way through miles and miles of pipes, their spirits low. Sunshine tried to put on a brave face. "I'm sure there's raccoon heaven just above our heads," he said. "A land of comfy sofas and unlimited food."

A flood of sewage cascaded down behind them, drenching the raccoons in smelly goo.

"Then again, maybe not," groaned Rocky. "I'm getting out at the next exit. Whatever's up there can't be as bad as what we're putting up with down here!"

At the next shaft of light, Rocky was as good as his word, standing on Dempsey's shoulders and sliding the iron grate to the side. He heaved himself out into the daytime, his sensitive eyes blinking in the light. He didn't know it, but he was in a school playground. *So many tiny human beings,* he marveled as they skipped and ran all around him.

"There he is!" exclaimed a little girl. "I told you so, Mylie. There's my raccoon with pants on. He had breakfast at my house." Before he knew what was happening, Rocky was scooped up into the little girl's arms and cradled like a baby. "Pooee, my baby's a bit stinky. I think he needs his diaper changed."

Rocky struggled, but the little girl was used to having a cat, so her grip was tight. There was soon a crowd around her, and a hundred little fingers poked and prodded the raccoon. "Stop, you're tickling," chuckled Rocky, "but I like it." Before he knew what was happening, a whistle had blown and Rocky had been stuffed into the little girl's bag and taken into school. "Quiet in there, baby," she whispered. "I'll bathe you when we get home. And I'm going to call you... Angelina."

Rocky was resigned to his fate. He'd lost the will to struggle. He wasn't too pleased with his new name, but he'd enjoyed the cuddle and a bath would be most welcome. *Things were looking up!*

Rocky's gang had watched the little girl kidnap him. They peered through the window as their poor, defenseless pal was stuffed into a pink backpack. "It's got ponies on it," wailed Dempsey. "And he *hates* ponies."

It wasn't long before the gang felt themselves coming full circle. They waited in a tree, watching for the pink pony bag until the school bell rang and kids poured out of school. "There are hundreds of pink pony bags," wailed Dempsey.

"There she is," spied Quickpaw, as the little girl walked slowly to her dad's Jeep, cradling the bag in her arms.

"Wait...isn't this the car we hitched a ride in earlier?" asked Sunshine as the three raccoons slipped unnoticed into the back of the vehicle and stowed away in last night's sleeping bag.

CHAPTER 11

Drainpipe Pete

Quickpaw watched the little girl swinging her pink pony bag as she skipped up the path to the yard. "We're a gang of four," he said gravely, "and Rocky is in terrible danger."

"Doesn't look like danger to me," piped up Dempsey. "That little girl was cuddling him."

"Don't be fooled. There's nothing more dangerous than humans," glared Quickpaw. "Rocky needs us." The friends huddled together and Quickpaw pointed to the chimney as he explained the plan.

The man looked puzzled. Twelve hours earlier he'd been hunting in the forest and a pair of raccoons had caused one of his friends to step into a trap and another to take a great fall. And, it was the strangest thing, but one of the animals was wearing pants. Then, his morning had been turned upside down, having to clean up after his little girl who'd made a terrific mess. Plus, she'd drawn a picture of a pants-wearing raccoon. It was almost as if the creature was haunting him! So when his little girl opened her pony backpack and plucked out a tired critter, wearing very dirty underpants, he dropped his coffee in shock. "Daddy, I want to introduce you to Angelina." A strong smell of tuna filled the air and some pepperoni fell out of the pants.

"Good evening," waved Rocky. "No wonder you look shocked, sir. I can explain. You're not seeing me at my best. Your little girl's right, I probably need a bath. And can we think of a better name than Angelina?"

The man grabbed Rocky by the foot and started to drag him to the door. His little girl began to scream—and this was the moment the rescue kicked in. Sunshine slid down the banister, shooting off the end and careening into the man, causing him to drop Rocky. *Ooof!* There was soot everywhere. Dempsey was next, getting a running start on the wooden floor before launching himself on his furry belly. He skidded into the man, knocking him over, ten-pin-bowling style. "Strike!"

Quickpaw appeared at the door, standing tall. Rocky blinked hard. His friend was wearing one of the little girl's red T-shirts around his neck, like a cape. "Quickpaw Cassidy at your service," he grinned. "This superhero has come to save you, Angelin—I mean Rocky."

"B-B-But I don't need saving," stammered Rocky. "I was just going to have a nice warm bath. I live here, I think."

The man was getting to his feet. He lunged at Rocky and grabbed at the raccoon's waistband. "Come here, varmint!" he yelled. "You're responsible for my friend being in the hospital!"

"Sorry, old boy," shrieked Quickpaw. "I hate to do this, but—" he sank his teeth into the man's hand and then let go, Rocky yelping as the waistband slapped his bottom—"you have to release my friend."

The raccoons were off through the cat-flap, dashing across the lawn. They skipped under the ripped trampoline and back into the nearest storm drain, then sat, panting. Nobody said it, but they were all thinking the same thing. *The city isn't all it's cracked up to be.*

The next day it was raining heavily. Only once did the raccoons venture out into the gray cityscape. They found some garbage bags in a dark alley and rummaged through them hungrily, but Rocky could only find some morsels of moldy bread and cold chicken wings. Dempsey found the best meal, a half-eaten doggie bag. Quickpaw sniffed around, but he didn't really have an appetite. Rocky sat in a doorway gnawing on a bone. "The streets aren't exactly 'paved with food,'" he grumbled. Sunshine, usually so positive, could find little to smile about as he chewed on a rain-sodden pizza crust.

The raccoons heard rustling nearby and looked up. A pair of yellow eyes peered at them out of the gloom. Then another pair. And another. Rocky dropped his bone and backed away down the alley. He looked around and noticed hundreds of eyes gleaming in the grayness. Several large city rats emerged into the rain. The Hole-in-the-Tree gang snapped to attention—they knew rats had a fearsome reputation. Quickpaw tried to look bigger than he actually was, but it was clear that the raccoons were heavily outnumbered. He growled at the rats, but they kept advancing. Dempsey threw his food at the enemy and the four raccoons scampered down the alley. Rats were coming from all angles. "We're surrounded!" he shrieked. "What's the plan?"

Quickpaw led by example. He'd calculated that rats were fast, cunning, and evil, but they weren't great climbers. He leaped onto a pile of boxes and then onto a wire fence. The gang followed, clinging on with their raccoon fingers. They followed their leader upward as far as the first floor and then joined him in a giant leap onto a balcony. From there it was easier. They felt like raccoons again, but instead of branches, they were swinging effortlessly on drainpipes, railings, and window ledges. The rats were long gone.

Quickpaw was the first to reach the highest point of the city. It was a cold and cloudy afternoon. The rain slanted sideways, painting the city with an extra shade of gray. The raccoon shivered, his fur damp and floppy, and his whiskers drooping as low as his shoulders. Before long his friends joined him, four soaked raccoons staring out over miles and miles of endless concrete. Rocky sobbed. No words were necessary.

The bedraggled gang eventually returned to the safety of the tunnels. They sat watching rain dripping through a grate, the misery summing up their mood. Sunshine nudged Dempsey. Bright eyes shone in the tunnel ahead. "Probably another rat," hissed Sunshine. "But it looks like there's only one. Stay together and we'll be okay. Chances are, he'll be more scared of us than we are of him."

Rocky wasn't so sure. The beady eyes glowed closer as the Hole-in-the-Tree gang huddled together in the smelly goo. The stranger passed under a rare shaft of light. "You're a raccoon," exclaimed Dempsey, sounding startled.

The stranger felt himself all over, as if checking the fact. "Sure am, little buddy," replied the raccoon. "Always have been. They call me Drainpipe Pete 'cause I was born and raised down here. A city slicker raccoon if ever there was one." Drainpipe Pete grinned a near-toothless grin. They noticed his white fur was more gray than white.

The other raccoons were in awe. "So you know where all the comfy shelter is?" gabbled Dempsey. "And the unlimited supplies of food?"

Drainpipe Pete rubbed his skinny belly. He stood under the light where the others could see his bony ribs sticking out of his chest. "Unlimited food, you say," he chuckled. "Here in the city we compete with humans, dogs, cats and—" he said, putting his paw to the side of his mouth and lowering his voice to a whisper—"rats."

He looked left and right before continuing. "And 'cause us raccoons is bottom of the pile, we only get what's left. Scraps, you hear. That's all we get."

"Oh," said Quickpaw, sounding a little deflated. "So why do you stay?"

Drainpipe Pete paused, as if that thought had never crossed his mind. "Stay? Well, I guess I don't know anything else, fellas," he admitted. "I know every stretch of these pipes and tunnels. But I have a dream. The same dream that every city raccoon shares."

The Hole-in-the-Tree gang looked at him expectantly.

Drainpipe Pete took off his little backpack and snapped it open. He took out a small picture and carefully opened it.

"My pop gave me this, just before he died. Says it's out there somewhere," smiled Drainpipe Pete. "It's every raccoon's dream."

Quickpaw, Sunshine, Rocky, and Dempsey strained to look at the picture.

"Wow," gasped Dempsey. "It's sooo beautiful." The raccoons stared at the magazine clipping of a forest. *Their forest!* It was shot from above so they could see a tall redwood canopy sitting alongside a lake with a small town clinging to the shore.

"The promised land," sighed the city slicker. "That's where you find unlimited freedom, fresh air, and food. And the legend has it," he began, gathering the gang together, "that the forest raccoons actually live in trees!"

"No way," gasped Dempsey.

"Yup, trees, I tell ya."

"I've heard that too, Drainpipe," said Quickpaw, sensing an opportunity here, "but can you tell us how to get to this raccoon heaven?"

"Nope," whistled the old raccoon through the gap in his teeth. "All I know is that some of the birds we speak to tell of this far-off land. Too far for us slickers to go. So we make do with this," he smiled, waving his hand around the sewer. "And this," he reminded them, pointing to his ribs.

"Anyways, cubs," he whistled, "nice speakin' to yuz. Old Drainpipe Pete has to go upstairs for summin' to eat." The city raccoon splashed around the bend, leaving the bedraggled and sagging Hole-in-the-Tree gang behind.

"I'm homesick," admitted Rocky. "I think we've made a massive mistake," he continued, speaking aloud what everyone else was thinking. "We had paradise and lost it. We had everything we needed and didn't realize it! We wanted more, more, more. We stole from Max and the villagers.

More food. Comfier living. Bigger pizzas. More fish. And all we got was this!" He waved his paw around the tunnel. "Less, less, less. Less food, less comfort, less sunshine. And," he sobbed, "even worse, less happiness."

"The city isn't quite how I imagined it," agreed Dempsey. "The pictures looked good. But the trees look better."

All of a sudden, Rocky was feeling brave. He stood tall and pulled his pants high. "I don't care how far it is. We made it here. We can make it home."

CHAPTER 12

Paradise Found

Hope turned into energy. All of a sudden the raccoons felt more upbeat, spurred on by the dream of returning to the forest. Yet every drain they opened led to more gray concrete. And every time they surfaced, the sky pelted them with rain. Dempsey stood forlornly outside an electronics store, his wet fur making him look scrawny. Rain dripped down the windows. Inside he could see the brand-new TVs and one was showing the news channel. Rivers were swollen and the weather lady, doing an outside broadcast, looked like she was getting blown away. He couldn't hear the words and wouldn't have understood them if he could, but Dempsey guessed that what she was saying was bad. These were the worst storms to hit the city in a very long time.

That evening the gang huddled in the least smelly tunnel. Dempsey had found an umbrella and was experimenting by flicking it up and down again. He wasn't sure what it was, but it was fun to play with. What the raccoons didn't know was that up above them, the rain had been falling for twenty-four hours. They'd noticed the water level rising, but thought nothing of it. Rain was bouncing off the streets and swirling into the storm drains. Rivers of water were gathering underneath the city, keeping the humans safe by swishing the problem underground.

It came at the Hole-in-the-Tree gang in a massive wave. Quickpaw was the first to sense it, a sort of sloshing sound in the tunnel behind them, like an eerie echo. He signaled to Dempsey to stop messing with the umbrella. "Listen," he said. "Water— and lots of it!"

And then they saw it, a wall of sludge, forcing its way through the underground tunnel. The raccoons began to run. Rocky turned to look behind and fell, splashing head first into the mess. Quick-thinking Quickpaw grabbed Dempsey's umbrella. "All aboard," he yelled, pressing the catch and letting the umbrella bloom. "This is our only chance!"

Sunshine nodded. There was no plan B, C, or D. If Plan A failed, they'd be drowned. The raccoons huddled together in the upturned umbrella and waited as the wall of water bore down on them. Then they were floating, swishing, and sloshing their way through the darkness like the best fair ride in the world. The umbrella's short handle sometimes caught on the low roof, creating sparks that lit the way. Quickpaw was enjoying it. "*Woohoo!*" he barked, "What a way to travel." Eventually, even Rocky peeped out from behind his paws.

After swooping downward and around many twists and turns, a small chunk of light appeared ahead. "Land ahoy!" yelled Quickpaw, pointing at the light. "I think the fun's about to end." The light got bigger until eventually the upturned umbrella shot out of the end of the drain, spitting the raccoons into the swirling river. Rocky was tipped out of the makeshift boat and splashed around before his friends hauled him back into the umbrella. The river calmed and their boat floated gently downstream. Rocky lay back and looked up at the trees. "We've made it, guys," he purred. "We're on our way back to the promised land."

The raccoons stayed afloat until they reached a quiet stretch of water farther downstream. They paddled to the shore and climbed out of their umbrella boat, sending it on its way.

"Trees!" gasped Rocky, hugging the nearest one. "I've missed you so very much."

"What now?" asked Dempsey.

"My granddad used to say that the first rule of raccoon survival is 'Always follow the stream.' And if this is our stream, we'll eventually find our way home," suggested Sunshine.

"But which way?" asked Dempsey.

Quickpaw looked up at the watery sun. He looked back at the drain they'd shot out of and calculated where the city was. His sharp raccoon mind put the pieces together in an instant. He raised his paw and pointed upstream. "That-a-way."

CHAPTER 13

Mad Max

It was a three-day trek. They slept by day and walked by night because it felt safer that way. They fished. And played. The raccoons were glad to be back in the forest, so much in fact that Rocky had become a tree hugger. "I love you, Mr. Oak," he said, kissing its bark. "And you too, Mrs. Elm," he smooched, grasping the tree in his arms.

The gang came across a family having a picnic and Quickpaw resisted the urge to carry out another heist. "It was stealing that got us into this mess," he said. "So our robbing days are over. Fish, grubs, and fruit, that's what raccoons eat. That's what city slickers dream of. And that's what we're going to eat from now on. Agreed?"

"Agreed," chorused the gang, scampering past an open picnic basket.

Rocky saw the village first. He'd run ahead to climb a tree. He found the biggest

redwood he could see and clawed his way to the top. *What a view!* And down below, about half a mile away, was their lake. He squinted to see the detail. *And Max's store! "Woohoo!"* they heard from above. "We're home!"

The rest of the gang joined Rocky at the top of the redwood. Sure enough, laid out below was the picture from Drainpipe Pete's magazine. "That, my friends," gasped Dempsey, "is raccoon paradise."

"Except, we have no home," reminded Rocky. "It was toppled, remember? And there are 'Wanted' posters with our faces on them. And Max has a posse after us. And—"

"And speaking of Max," interrupted Quickpaw, "what's happening at the store?"

The raccoons squinted into the distance. A black van had just pulled up outside Max's store. They could tell it had arrived quickly because there was a dust cloud where it had stopped. A man in a hoodie burst inside Max's store. They strained to see the action unfold below. Max fell out of the door, tumbling onto his back in the dirt, while the hooded man stood over the storekeeper and appeared to hit him!

The gang shimmied down the tree. "Max is in trouble," shouted Rocky. "He needs our help!"

By the time the raccoons got to the village, all was quiet. The black van was still parked there, but Max's store had the "Closed for lunch" sign hanging from the door handle. *Strange*, thought Sunshine. *It's too early for lunch.*

Quickpaw went first, his red T-shirt-cape billowing behind. He peered through the mail slot and saw that Max was tied to a chair and his mouth was gagged with socks. Max saw the black raccoon eyes. He said nothing, but Quickpaw knew that look—the old man was pleading for help. Rocky watched from the window as the hooded man helped himself to the bills and coins that were in the drawer that he'd hidden in. He was stuffing them into a bag.

The raccoons knew what was happening. They'd broken into Max's General Store several times, but never wanted to do any harm to the old man. Mostly they escaped with a few morsels of food and Max hadn't even known they'd been there. This was much worse!

Quickpaw was working on a plan— and he knew he didn't have long. He sent Dempsey into the forest with clear instructions to look for something. He shook the door handle of the van and swung it open. He removed the baseball bat from the passenger seat and handed it to Quickpaw, who gripped it tightly and did a couple of practice swings.

The raccoons instinctively knew what to do next. They weren't a gang, they were a team. No words were necessary.

The robber unlocked the front door and sauntered out, trying to look casual. Rocky was perched on the roof and was on him in a flash, gripping tightly, his dirty underpants in the man's face and his claws up the robber's nose. The man was confused and in pain. He lashed out at the raccoon and as he did so, Quickpaw swung the bat at the robber's

THWACK!

shins. The man fell, clutching his legs in agony. He looked around frantically, only to see a raccoon in underpants dancing a jig and another wearing a cape and bringing a baseball bat down onto his head. *Clonk!* The robber was dazed, but not knocked out. He staggered to his feet, dropped his money bag, and hobbled to his van. He turned the key and the engine roared.

Sunshine stepped back and retracted his sharp claws, proud of his handiwork. *Deflating all four tires down in less than two minutes is quite an achievement.*

The van started to pull away, its wheels spinning and the robber struggling to grip the steering wheel. Meanwhile, Dempsey returned, carrying the police walkie-talkie in his paw. He bounded through the store door and removed the socks from Max's mouth. He clicked the walkie-talkie button and waited for Max to speak. "Erm, hello," started the old man, "police? Is that Marvin at the station?"

"Sure is," crackled the radio. "Who's this speaking on our stolen radio?"

"It's Max," said Max, "from the general store."

"You stole our radio?" asked the policeman.

"No, I didn't steal your radio," spat the storekeeper, "but I do want to report something stolen. My money! There's a robbery taking place right here, *right now!*"

The burglar had given up way before the police car caught up with his van. He was sitting on a curb, his tires shredded. When the policeman read the robber his rights, in response to "Anything you say can and will be used against you..." he babbled on and on about superhero raccoons ruining his day.

It was almost exactly a week later that the raccoons made their formal apology to Max. The old man opened the door, his head still bandaged, and stepped outside like he always did. He breathed in the fresh mountain air, like he always did. And there, on his doorstep, was a bathmat and a pair of pants. And inside the pants was a freshly caught salmon. Max looked around. He couldn't see the raccoons, but he knew they were out there. The storekeeper bent down and picked up the fish. He smiled. Underneath the salmon were some coins and a pineapple chunk. "A peace offering from them varmints," grinned the old man.

Max looked out into the forest and waved at the redwood trees. He knew he and the Hole-in-the-Tree gang were quits.

CHAPTER 14

Community Service

Smoke billowed from the barbecue and the smell of cooking wafted through the air. Dempsey lapped his milkshake and then stood on his hind legs, stretching to see the barbecuing fish. His white whiskers twitched and he rubbed his tummy in anticipation. *This time I'll be getting a piece of the action.* He looked at the scene. The village folk were standing around, chatting and drinking. McCluskey was swinging in Max's hammock.

Rocky was wearing bright white underpants. He loved them and was delighted to have been given a fresh pair to wear every day. He always saved his Superman ones for Saturdays. He loved the superhero look and besides, it kept the attention away from his missing tail. He'd struck up a friendship with Max's granddaughter and was often seen being wheeled around the village in a baby carriage. "Shame on you," taunted

Dempsey, peering at Rocky, dressed in a bonnet, but Rocky didn't care. When the little girl picked him up and cuddled him so hard he squeaked, Dempsey couldn't help feeling a tiny bit jealous.

Quickpaw Cassidy looked down from his new den. It was a fine redwood with a superb view of the village. Each member of the Hole-in-the-Tree gang had his own bedroom complete with cushions that had been donated rather than stolen. Rocky's spare pants were folded neatly in the corner and this time there was no skyscraper wallpaper. He could hear Sunshine's gentle snoring coming from his room. *Relaxing again!*

Quickpaw surveyed the scene below
in which happy villagers went about
their daily business. Beyond them, the

lake shimmered and the river twisted into the distance. Quickpaw knew that somewhere over the horizon was the big city. He took a deep breath of fresh mountain air and puffed out his chest with pride. As leader, his first responsibility had always been to look after the safety of his gang. *And keep their tummies full*, he chuckled, watching Dempsey scamper off with a plate of salmon.

The villagers had been so grateful to the raccoons for coming to Max's assistance that all grudges had been forgotten. Quickpaw wasn't sure if the truce would be permanent, but it felt good while it lasted. He thought back to their time in the city. *Enough adventures*, he concluded. *At least for a while.*

 # Wildlife Reader's Club

Join today at
www.barronsbooks.com/series/awesome

Join our **Wildlife Reader's Club**
for the latest news on your favorite
Awesome Animals, plus:

- A club certificate and membership card
- Wildlife games, activities, puzzles, and coloring pages
- Excerpts from the books and news about forthcoming titles
- Contests for **FREE** stuff

Open to U.S. residents only.

Visit **www.barronsbooks.com/series/awesome**
today and join in the fun!